The African Grasslands

Alan Trussell-Cullen

The African Grasslands

Fast Forward
Turquoise Level 17

Text: Alan Trussell-Cullen
Editor: Johanna Rohan
Design: Vonda Pestana
Series design: James Lowe
Production controller: Seona Galbally
Photo research: Gillian Cardinal
Audio recordings: Juliet Hill, Picture Start
Spoken by: Matthew King and Abbe Holmes
Reprint: Jennifer Foo

Acknowledgements
The author and publisher would like to acknowledge permission to reproduce material from the following sources: Photographs by Age Fotostock/Werner Bollmann, p8 top/John Glover, p23 right; Auscape International/Ferrero Labat, pp 4-5/BSIP, p23 top; Getty Images/Beverly Joubert, front cover centre/Photodisc/Tom Brakefield, pp 12-13 top/Wolhuter Media, pp 12-13 bottom/Kim Wolhuter, p20/ J Sneesby/B Wilkins, p21/Eastcott Momatiuk; istockphoto, Pauline Wilson, p10/Norma Reid, p11/Andy Green, p17 bottom/Derek Demmann, back cover, p18 bottom; Photolibrary/Mark Deeble & Victoria Stone, p6/Hilary Pooley, p8 bottom/Robert Francis, pp 3, 9/Mark Boulton, p14/David Paynter, p15/ifa-Bilderteam Gmbh, p16/John Downer, pp 17 top, 19 bottom/Paul Goldstein, pp 18-19 top.

ISBN 978 0 17 012630 4
ISBN 978 0 17 012621 2 (set)

Cengage Learning Australia
Level 7, 80 Dorcas Street
South Melbourne, Victoria Australia 3205
Phone: 1300 790 853

Cengage Learning New Zealand
Unit 4B Rosedale Office Park
331 Rosedale Road, Albany, North Shore NZ 0632
Phone: 0800 449 725

For learning solutions, visit **cengage.com.au**

Printed in Australia by Ligare Pty Ltd
2 3 4 5 6 7 8 22 21 20 19 18

Evaluated in independent research by staff from the Department of Language, Literacy and Arts Education at the University of Melbourne.

Evaluated in independent research by staff from the Department of Language, Literacy and Arts Education at the University of Melbourne.

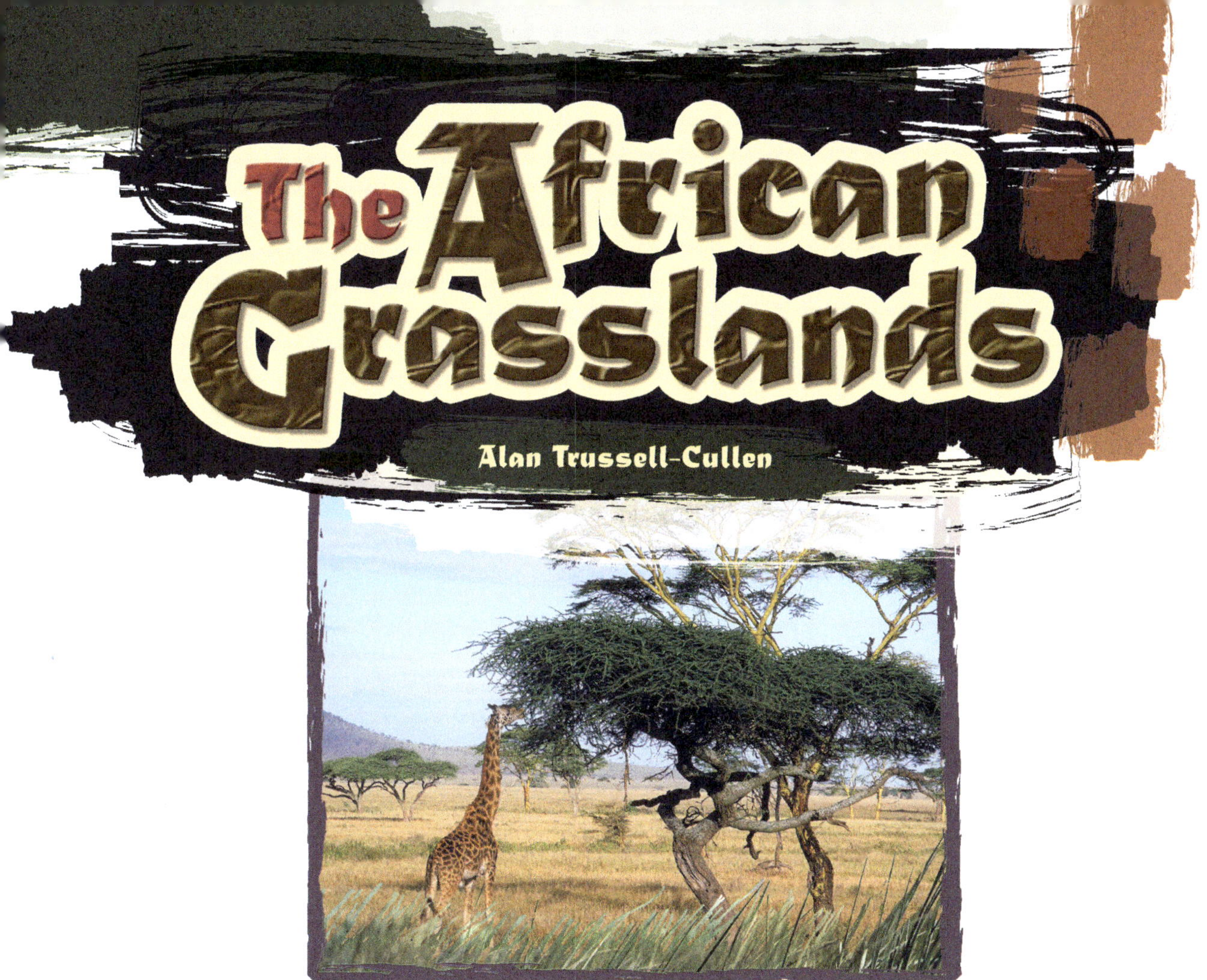

Contents

Chapter 1

THE AFRICAN GRASSLANDS' FOOD CHAIN

The African grasslands are close to the **equator**, where it's hot all year.
It rains there for part of the year, and for the rest of the year it's very hot and dry.

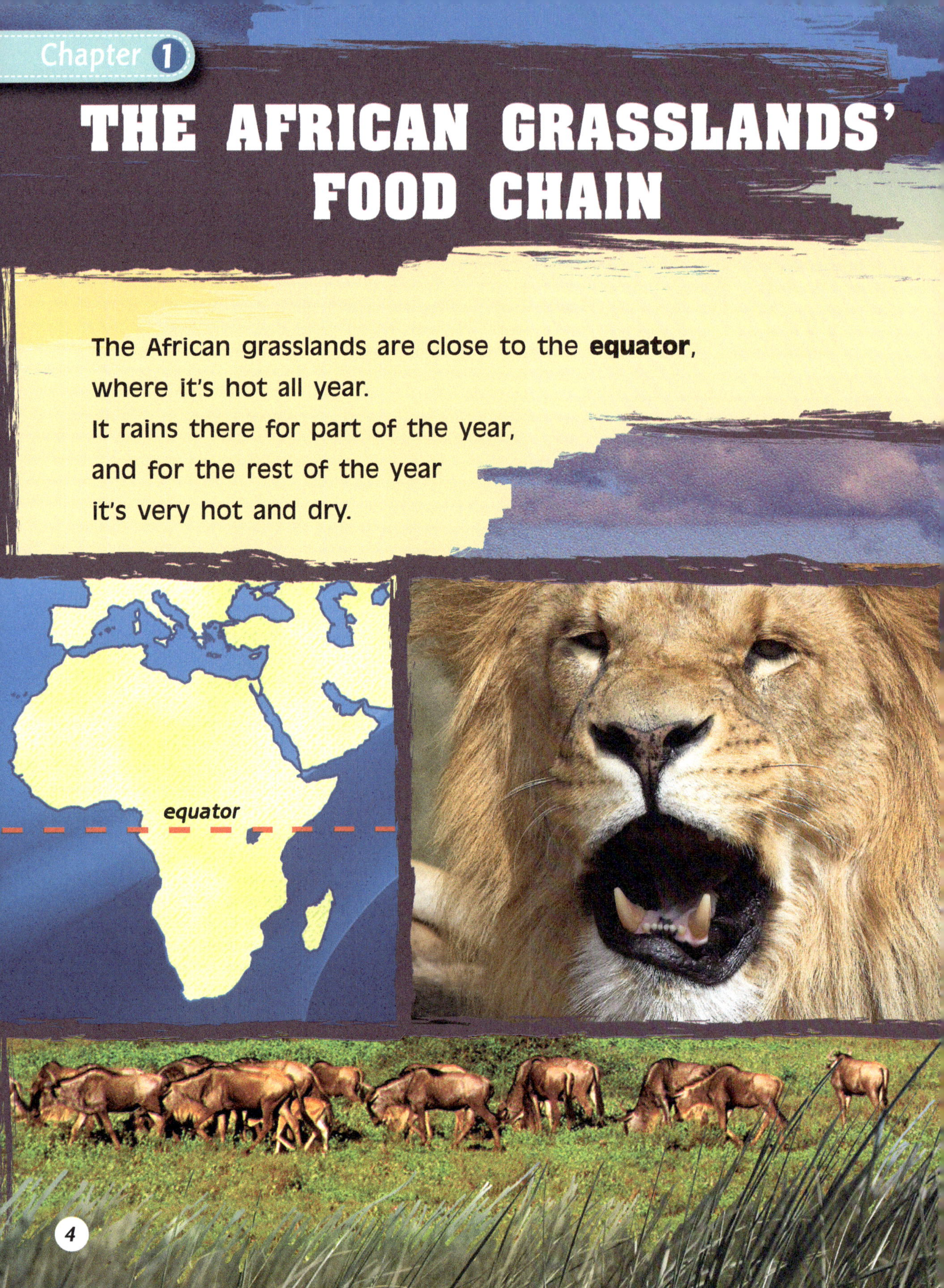

Many kinds of plants and animals live in the African grasslands.

Food links all living things in this **habitat**, and together all these links make up a food chain.

Chapter 2

PLANTS

Plants are the first link in the food chain. Plants are the only living things that can make their own food.

Plants make food from water and **carbon dioxide** using **chlorophyll** in their leaves and energy from the Sun.

Plants are called **producers** because they produce food.

Grass is an important producer in the African grasslands' food chain. It grows quickly when it's wet and survives most of the year when it's very hot and dry.

In the African grasslands,
there is not enough rain throughout the year
for forests to grow.
But, some trees and bushes can survive.

baobab trees

Running Words 161

Most of the trees in the African grasslands
are acacias.
They often look flat on top.
Giraffes eat the leaves from below.

Baobab trees also grow in the African grasslands.
They can store lots of water
in the soft wood of their trunks.

Chapter 3

PLANT-EATING ANIMALS

Animals need food for energy, but they can't make their own food. Animals get their food from plants or from other animals that eat plants. Animals are called **consumers**.

Plant-eating animals, like elephants, are the second link in the food chain. They are called primary consumers.

Zebras and wildebeest are also primary consumers. They can often be seen in the African grasslands eating grass near each other.

The grass in the African grasslands goes brown and stops growing in the driest part of the year.

When this happens, animals go to look for food in other places.

Each year up to 1.5 million wildebeest set out on a long journey to find food. They return when the rains come again.

Many plant-eating animals have body parts that help them get food. The giraffe uses its long neck to reach the high leaves of the acacia trees. Other animals can't reach this high.

Elephants are huge animals,
and need lots of food.
They have long trunks
that are good for
reaching and grabbing food.
They also have teeth and strong jaws
that are good for crushing plants.
They eat grass, flowers, leaves, and bark.

PREDATORS

Predators are the third link in the food chain. They are called secondary consumers because they get their food from eating other animals.

a leopard

a lion

Leopards, hyenas and lions are predators in the African grasslands' food chain.

a hyena

Lions live in groups called prides.

There can be up to 25 lions in a pride.

It's usually the job of the female lions in the pride to hunt.

Females hunt in groups at night.

Lions prey on animals that aren't as fast as them, like wildebeest, zebras and antelopes. They have pointed teeth to grip and tear their **prey**.

Leopards hunt at night, like lions. They prey on the same animals as lions, and also on reptiles and birds.

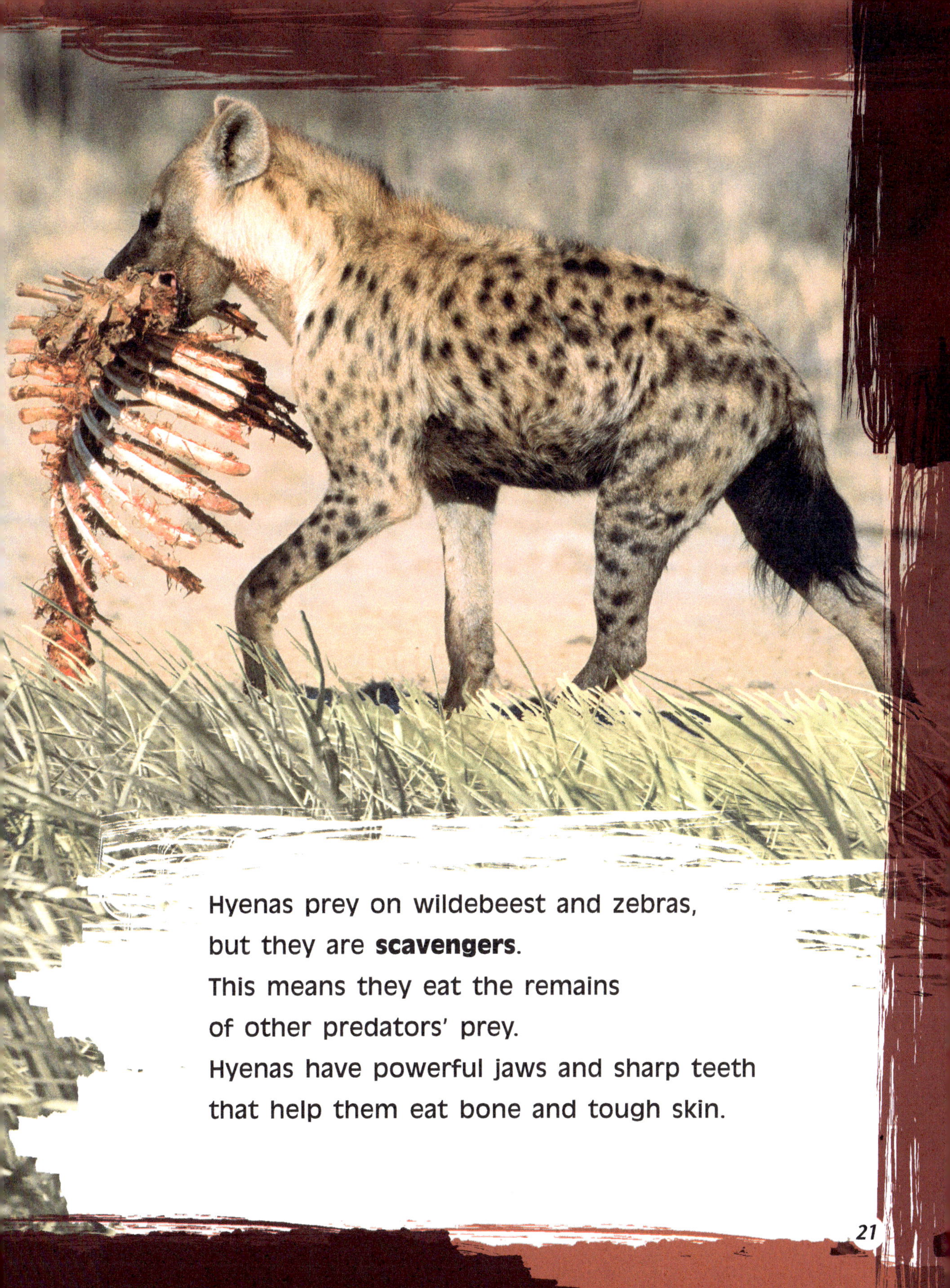

Hyenas prey on wildebeest and zebras, but they are **scavengers**. This means they eat the remains of other predators' prey. Hyenas have powerful jaws and sharp teeth that help them eat bone and tough skin.

DECOMPOSERS

Decomposers are the final link in the African grasslands' food chain.

Decomposers such as bacteria, fungi and worms help to break down dead plant and animal material. This material goes back into the soil to help plants grow.

bacteria
earthworms

Glossary

carbon dioxide a colourless, odourless gas

chlorophyll a green pigment found in plants that helps them absorb energy from the Sun

consumers animals that consume plants and other animals for food energy

decomposers bacteria, fungi and worms that break down dead plant and animal materials

equator an imaginary line on the Earth dividing it into the northern and southern hemispheres

habitat the natural home or environment of an animal

predators animals that eat other animals

producers things that make something

prey animals eaten by predators

scavengers animals that eat dead animals

Index